The
Little Hen

Written by Judy Nayer
Illustrated by Ron LeHew

The little hen wanted to make a cake.
"Will you help me?" she asked.

2

"Not I!" said the big dog.

"Not I!" said the pet cat.

"Not I!" said the red fox.

3

"Then I will do it myself."

"Will you help me now?" asked the little hen.

"Not I!" said the big dog.

"Not I!" said the pet cat.

"Not I!" said the red fox.

5

"Then I will do it myself."

"Will you help me now?" asked the little hen.

"Yes!" said the big dog.

"Yes!" said the pet cat.

"Yes!" said the red fox.

"No!" said the little hen.
"I will do it all by myself!"